FIREHOUSE DOG

Adapted by DANIELLE DENEGA

from the screenplay written by
CLAIRE-DEE LIM & MIKE WERB
& MICHAEL COLLEARY

Cartwheel
·B·O·O·K·S· ®

SCHOLASTIC INC.

New York Toronto London Auckland Sydney
Mexico City New Delhi Hong Kong Buenos Aires

REGENCY ENTERPRISES PRESENTS A NEW REGENCY PRODUCTION A TODD HOLLAND FILM "FIREHOUSE DOG" JOSH HUTCHERSON BRUCE GREENWOOD DASH MIHOK STEVEN CULP BILL NUNN MUSIC SUPERVISOR PATRICK HOULIHAN MUSIC BY JEFF CARDONI CO-PRODUCER MICHAEL J. MASCHIO FILM EDITOR SCOTT JAMES WALLACE PRODUCTION DESIGNER TAMARA DEVERELL DIRECTOR OF PHOTOGRAPHY VICTOR HAMMER PRODUCED BY MICHAEL COLLEARY AND MIKE WERB WRITTEN BY CLAIRE-DEE LIM & MIKE WERB & MICHAEL COLLEARY DIRECTED BY TODD HOLLAND

PG | PARENTAL GUIDANCE SUGGESTED ⊚
SOME MATERIAL MAY NOT BE SUITABLE FOR CHILDREN ®
Sequences of Action Peril,
Some Mild Crude Humor and Language.

www.firehousedogmovie.com

©2006 Twentieth Century Fox

ISBN-13: 978-0-439-89643-6
ISBN-10: 0-439-89643-6

© 2007 Regency Entertainment (USA), Inc. in the U.S.
© 2007 Monarchy Enterprises S.a.r.l. in the rest of the world.

Published by Scholastic Inc.
SCHOLASTIC and associated logos are trademarks and/or registered trademarks of Scholastic Inc.

12 11 10 9 8 7 6 5 4 3 2 1   7 8 9 10/0

Printed in the U.S.A.
First printing, February 2007

There was once a famous movie star who could do amazing stunts and tricks.
But this movie star was different.
He was a dog! His name was Rex.

One day, Rex was filming a movie stunt inside an airplane. But there was an accident, and he fell out.

Luckily, Rex fell right into a truck full of tomatoes. He did not get hurt, but he did smell funny.

Rex's owner and manager was a man named Trey.

After the accident, Trey looked everywhere for Rex. But he could not find his special dog.

"I was supposed to take care of him!" Trey cried.

Rex was scared and alone.
A scary animal control officer tried to capture him.
"Oh, yeah, you're mine," he said.
But Rex escaped.

The same day, a boy named Shane crossed paths with Rex.

Shane was cutting school that day. He and Rex ran right into each other.

Rex burped in Shane's face. Gross!

"I hate that dog," Shane said.

Then Rex ran off.

He was tired from his scary day and needed some rest. He found an empty building and took a nap.

What Rex did not know was that someone was about to set the building on fire. . . .

Shane's dad, Connor, was a fire captain at Dogpatch Station.

When he found out that Shane was cutting school again, he got very angry.

"How many times did I warn you about ditching?" he asked his son.

Just then, a fire alarm sounded. The Dogpatch
firefighters jumped into action, but they were too slow.
They were the last firefighters to arrive at the scene.
They were always coming in last lately.

Shane stayed safely in the fire truck and watched his dad rush inside the burning building.

He was scared that Connor would get hurt.

Then Shane spotted something on the roof of the building. It was a trapped dog!

Shane pointed to the dog.

"Dad! Dad! Look! Up there!" he called.

Connor climbed up and rescued the animal.

Shane realized it was the same smelly dog that he had seen earlier that day. He named the dog Dewey. He did not know that the dog's real name was Rex.

Shane's dad was worried. There had been a lot of fires recently. He had a theory. He thought the fires were all being set on purpose.

Nevertheless, Zack Hayden, the city manager, told Connor that the fire station might have to be shut down soon.

It was because the firefighters were not doing as good a job as they could.

That night, Shane brought Dewey home with him. He made posters with Dewey's picture on them to hang up around town.

The posters would help the dog's owner find him.

At Shane's house, Dewey began showing what a special dog he was.

He gave himself a bath . . .

. . . and he cleaned Shane's room.

"You are one strange dog," Shane said.

The next day, Dewey showed Shane more of his movie-star tricks.

Dewey rode Shane's skateboard and jumped over a moving car.

"What are you—some kind of circus dog?" Shane asked Dewey.

Shane brought Dewey to the firefighters' picnic to compete in the dog obstacle course. Dewey did an awesome job—until he spotted a beautiful Dalmatian named Sparky. She reminded Dewey of his last girlfriend and made him stop dead in his tracks. This cost him the win.

The Dogpatch fire company was very proud of Dewey, anyway.

"Sweetest thing I've seen in months," Firefighter Lionel said.

The next day, the Dogpatch firefighters reported to the scene of a collapsed tunnel.

A friend of Connor's was trapped inside. Shane's dad ran in to save his friend, but it was very dangerous. Luckily, Dewey came to the rescue! Shane's special new dog helped save the day.

After the rescue, Dewey and Shane's dad were on TV.

Dewey was famous again.

"Smile, Wonder Dog. You made the news," a reporter said to Dewey.

Dewey received so much attention that the mayor decided not to close down Dogpatch Station after all.

Shane's dad was pleased. He said, "Maybe all Dogpatch needed was a good dog."

Shane's dad kept investigating the fires he thought were being set on purpose.

Shane wanted to help, too. So he studied photos and reports from each fire.

Shane noticed that there was a watch in one picture. It had the brand name BOUTINE on it. Could that be a clue?

A few nights later, a fancy charity event was held in honor of all the local fire stations. Shane brought Dewey to perform a few tricks.

All the firefighters were there. Zack Hayden and a local businessman named Sellars were there, too.

In the audience, there was someone unexpected —
Trey!

"You found my dog!" he said to Shane and his dad.

Trey had seen his lost dog on television. He told them
Dewey's real name was Rex. Trey wanted his dog back.

"It's his dog, Shane. We don't have a choice," Connor
told his son.

Rex left with Trey, and Shane was very sad.

Then the Dogpatch firefighters had to leave the charity event to respond to another fire.

Back at Trey's hotel, Rex heard the sirens. He wanted to help.

Trey tried to calm Rex down. "Chill, dude, it's just a siren," he said.

But Rex ran away. He caught up with the Dogpatch fire engine and hopped on board.

Shane stayed at the charity event. He had noticed something that made him think: The businessman named Sellars was wearing a watch that said BOUTINE on it.

It was the same kind of watch Shane had seen in the fire reports!

Shane knew he was on to something important, so he followed Sellars.

Shane listened as Sellars told another man to set fire to a building.

Shane went to the Dogpatch Station right away. He had to tell his dad what he'd heard! But when Shane got to the station, no one was there. Then he heard something funny . . .

Zack Hayden was setting Dogpatch Station on fire! The city manager was the one setting fires all over town! Shane confronted Zack. "You did it!" Shane yelled as he sprayed him with fire retardant.

Meanwhile, the fire station exploded in flames—with Shane and Zack trapped inside!

From far away, Rex sensed that something was wrong.

Rex alerted Shane's dad to get back to the station. The Dogpatch firefighters rushed as fast as they could. When they arrived at the scene, the station was engulfed in flames.

But Rex ran right in and rescued Shane from the fire! After he was safe, Shane explained to his dad what he had seen. He knew that Sellars had asked Zack Hayden to burn down all the buildings. "He set the fires. All of them," Shane told Connor.

The next day, the whole town knew about Zack Hayden and Sellars. The police arrested them. And Dogpatch Station was given a special medal by the mayor.

Trey gave Rex to Shane to keep forever. "After being a real hero, he'd never be happy just acting like one," Trey said about Rex.

Rex became the official firehouse dog of Dogpatch Station.